REVELATIONS THE PROPHETS
BOOK ONE DUST

GEN 2:7 AND THE LORD GOD FORMED MAN OF THE DUST OF THE GROUND, AND BREATHED INTO HIS NOSTRILS THE BREATH OF LIFE, AND MAN BECAME A LIVING BEING.

Characters

I   O1- not much is known of this one. only that he seems to be sethur's own personal body guard and apparently the general in charge of all his armies. it would be wise **not** to cross his path.

II   Anak- 3 times the size of most normal men, this 'freak of nature' is quite the site to behold. spoken of as legend. his origin is cloudy at best, but more important than where or who he came from is where he will be and what he will do.

III   Ariel- older brother to zebuddah and one of two prophesied to walk the earth. he fights his calling, and wars within himself, searching for truth. it is this struggle that is at the heart of this story. through his walk and example many will live, though even in victory he may not.

IV   Bishlam- a very quiet and peaceful man. usually speaking though action, he is a man of few words. often used to mediate a situation, console, or mend. but do not be fooled by his subdued dimeaner. bishlam is no pushover.

V   Chloe- this prepubescent aviation prodigy can pilot anything designed to be piloted and in some cases things that aren't. she may be 'just a kid' but don't doubt her ability or heart. she has on occassion bailed out ariel, zebuddah, and the rest of the crew.

VI   Dalphon- from noble and royal blood to a former member of a secret elite military force, he now has a new purpose and vigor in life as he joins forces with the rebellion, he can more than hold his own. and as war continues, he indeed will play a key role in the how these different pieces will ultimately fall into place.

VII   Dara- a true nomad, tough as nails, always on the go and wise beyond her years (think triple digits) . she has been at the forefront and lead of many civil and sometimes not so civil uprisings. fighting the good fight for a great many years. wisdom is her middle name.

VIII   Elymas- there are few people more ruthless, manipulative, and cutthroat than warden elymas. it is said that no living person has actually seen him in person. he is the man behind hazar maveth (the last known prison on earth. if it can be called it a prison, it's more like slavery). always the opportunist he will go to great lengths (or rather make the inmates go to great lengths) to add to his already great amassing wealth and assets. if he endorses it, they WILL do it... or be under the ax for their insolence.

XI	**Guard-** elymas' elect few. men of gigantic stature. very few warriors of any world of any time could hold a candle to these souless brutes. said to be among the most feared group of enforcers ever essembled. they are in charge of keeping 'in check' the most dangerous criminals in the world. there are few who dare to oppose these seemingly heartless enforcers, and when those foolish do, the few become even fewer.
X	**Kedar-** a true man of valor. often putting other's welfare before his own (almost to a fault). he has helped more people in more ways than he will ever know. you'd be hard pressed to find a "gooder" samaritan.
XI	**Lotan-** few people in all this earth's history have played the role of antagonist better than sethur lotan. though he has the backing and support of the world's multitude, he represents the inverse of all of what the rebellion means and stands for. he has the favor of the public and the masses, and though he seemingly brings peace to the nations on the surface. he in actualllyity is perverting the truth and putting elements in play that he has no concept of... or does he?
XII	**Nerues-** a former government employee. who has now joined the rebellion in hopes to shed some light on a world that has grown dark, bleek, and dead. he is the salt and light of this earth... well, definitely the light.
XII	**Soldiers-** sethur's boys. the few the proud, trying to be all that they can be. their loyalty is only surpassed by their blind ignorance in following whatever he commands. though when together and in battle array, they are quite the admirable foe.
XIV	**Vashti-** from a very wild past and a rocky childhood. she is a prime example of finishing the race (life) strong. beatiful, dangerous, and deadly, though she has found a very novel way of handling that.
XV	**Zebuddah-** younger sister to ariel, and one of the two prophesied to come. she is the one that has kept ariel in line all these years and will seem to continue to do so, (because he really does seem to get into trouble quite frequently). raised on the word and an acclaimed biblical scholar. she is dead set on 'seeking and saving that which was lost' ...starting with her own big brother.

Prologus

In the not too distant future, the world is in great turmoil. it has become a wicked place immersed in darkness. countless suffer and starve, many grow sick and some sleep. meanwhile, a handful of individuals flourish and live lavishly only to feed their own greed and lust. they look down upon the weak and sadly, these "weak" are unable to stand for themselves. there is no unity, only division. thus spawning conflict and strife among the classes and countries. launching many outbreaks of civil unrest as terrorist acts run amok. tempers run hot in the middle east, and a the united nations step in, things only escalate. giving birth to what is properly dubbed "world war III" over time, and through many years and battles, one third of the world's population is depleted, germ warfare and the spreading of plagues completely changes the way of life and how people are now forced to live. new experimental vaccines are tried and tested, as well as gene manipulation, and much to their surprise with adverse unexpected results. all feel its effects, none are able to escape the dark clutches of this unholy war, that spans one hundred years from begining to end. only ceasing in the ashes of a nuclear climax. seemingly knocking all survivors back more than a few generations of progress. what few people that are left attempt to pick up the pieces, to find hope, move on and try to start again. however, engulfed in the dark shroud of the past, still looming above (a lingering reminder of all the death and destruction, like a bad aftertaste), they find themselves unchanged by the events which have just transpired. lost and without purpose, they try to find comfort in a sense of "normacy" they return to their ways of old.

Chapter One
Set apart

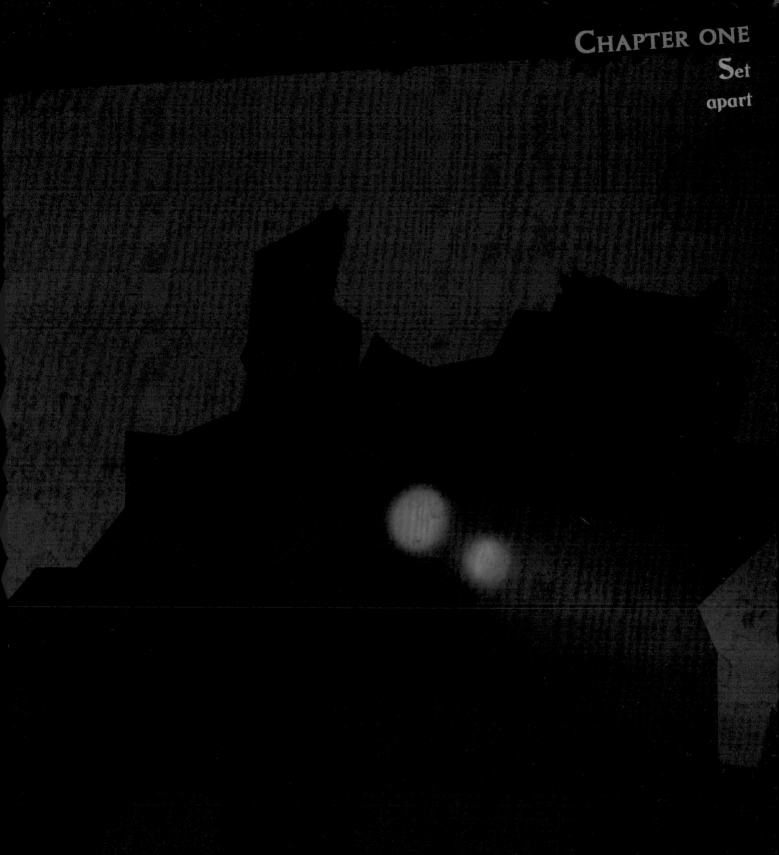

Thus the second woe begins... as two most unlikely candidates have been handpicked by the almighty Himself (unbeknownst to them). they shall be at the head of a great war, greater than any that has proceeded it. a battle is brewing, conflict raging, tides changing. such things have been put into motion and cannot be stopped. for soon, those without purpose shall find it, those without faith shall believe, those who are last shall become first, and those who are first shall become last. now those things which are temporal shall pass away, to reveal those things which are eternal. as the time for these prophets has come. they will war in this great war, fight the good fight, and they will fight well... however, this is a battle that they cannot win.

boooooooooom!

is it lotan's soldiers?

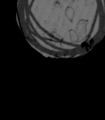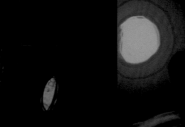

Chapter two
Dust
to dust

see what i mean?

there are more of them then there are of us... but they will USUALLY keep to themselves, just don't sleep on the ground.

?

SNAP! SQUEAK!

or, if you're like dara...and you're less than satisfied with the food services provided here...

i personally never get THAT hungry!

oh, yes, sorry bout' that. where are my manors?

the name's kedar. welcome to your new home away from home, hazar-maveth.

WHAT!?

other prisoner: shut up! and go to sleep!

coughs here?

exactly where in hell is "here" and who are you?

i've heard of this place before. i know what goes on here--

the only reason you're still alive, is because they feel you'd be a hard worker. they'd just as well enjoy seeing you six feet under, but since the dollar rules this world, you're just another dollar sign to them.

consider yourself blessed. you are among the crem de la crem of political outlaws religious zealots and mutant folk.

you don't know half of what goes on here.

i must get out of here... can you help?

is there a way?

in all my years here i have yet to find it... if i did, do you think that i would be here tonight talking to you this very moment?

if you knew anything of this place, you'd know of the stories that no one that has ever entered those dreary gates has ever exited them. many a person has stood where you stand now, and asked me those very same words, but alas, every last one of them is now dust, taking the long dirt nap.

every night i pray that the Lord will deliver me from this hell of a place

i guess that's one way to look at it.

no. for me it's the only way to look at it. there is purpose in everything

what's the hold up then?

...i feel that there is a purpose in all of this... that He has unfinished business for me, here.

hmmm... that voice is so familiar... but from where? a leg brace? could it be the "bossman" from the freakshow, so many years ago? but i thought him for dead... it can't be...so similar, but yet somehow different. after what happened i can't reveal myself to him.

what's wrong with your arm?

i was born with a condition...it doesn't work very well on it's own. they took all my equipment. i'm having problems, seeing and breathing in here.

?

here, i have something for you.

what's this?

the bandages will mend your arm and body, the book will mend you spirit and soul.

i'll see what i can do about getting your stuff back tomorrow. you're not going to be of much use to them if you can't work. and if you can't work you'll be fertilizer by day break.

thanks. i'll take the bandages for my arm, it should help... but i'm affraid i wouldn't make much use of this book. i think you have mistook me for my sister, she loves this kind of stuff. but, sorry. not for me.

on the contrary, that lil' book is the only reason that i have made it this far in THIS place... i tell you right now, this place can do crazy things to people, i have seen it happen time and time again. we think that the warden and guards are cruel and evil... they don't even compare to what this place can do to your mind, and then what your mind can do to you as a result.

in any event, i could go over passages in the scripture that have helped me... if you would like.

well... i don't know... i think for now i'll just hold on to it and give it a looksie' later on....

why you doing all of this for me anyways?

when i first got here, someone took me in and looked out for me. so lets just say i'm returning the favor...in their memory.

Many moons later...
over time ariel becomes one of hazar maveth's most diligent and successful workers, as warden elymas takes quite a liking to him (having big plans for his future). thus, ariel has become envied by many and been a marked man, on more than one occassion. but amazingly enough, he is respected and looked up to by even more of his fellow inmates. and as time has passed he has grown very close to kedar (finally realizing he is that same person, yet still not letting on that he was that kid that he took in, ashamed of the events which lead up to the separation and ultimatly to kedar's capture) much closer than before, much like a father son relationship. never more apparent than during the attempted prison escape from the mines of maveth. when a new batch of headstrong inmates plan a reckless break in a frantic attempt to free themselves from this "courtyard of death." as a result ariel and the rest find themselves caught in the middle, in the wrong place at the right time.

good work today in the fields. multiple treasures uncovered, not once, not twice, but thrice. and amazingly all by the same worker... ariel, you have the rest of the day off. enjoy it, you've earned it. however, the rest of you, almost a complete waste of a good day. you on the other hand have earned a glorious night of work in the mines... straight through til the morning, if need be, to make up for the total incompetence and lack of effort, you displayed today, and have shown on a consistant basis i might add.

very well. i'll never refuse a worker willing to work more. let that be an example to all of you! he is a TRUE worker. ariel stands head and shoulders above each and everyone of you. perhaps if you were even half the worker he was, my hand wouldn't be forced to terminate one of you every week.

sir, with all due respect. i regretedly must decline your gracious offer. i cannot in good concious, sit in my cell and rest while my fellow inmates are toiling away in the mines.

alright! you dogs heard the warden. get to work you worthless slugs!

"what now? ... this tunnel dead ends."

"not quite. this tunnel was closed and discontinued many years ago, because there was a miscalculation during the dig. about 1furlong past the supposed 'safe' zone, give or take. immediately every inmate involved in the dig was "X-ed" by remote downhere... even the guards on duty."

"wait a minute... how do you know all of this any how?"

"let's just say we have a very reliable source on the inside. now, if you don't mind, i would like to continue escaping!"

"sorry... just one last question..."

"what about these wonderful things around our necks?"

"yes. what is to stop warden elymas from making us meet the same end as those poor souls you just discribed in that story?"

"hey. you guys worry too much!"

"in any event, stay here, worry and think about it, if you want. we have some escaping to do."

"this is a very old facility and it's falling apart. the signal range sent by our colars is considerably weak. and grows weaker still. it doesn't reach down here. not anymore. that is."

"i don't trust them ariel.."

"ariel's right. we have to go with them. all we can do is pray that, we'll all make it through this."

"i don't either, dara. but it doesn't seem like we've got much of a choice."

the path forks ahead

i'm gonna say they went right.

muffled voices: hurry up, put some elbow grease into it already!

After coming to several hours later, with quite the throbbing headache and the lump to prove it. just as the dark guard had stripped him of all his gadgetry and was going to seal his cell, ariel inquired of the status of the others, and (not being the most sentimental of the guards) his words seem to fall apon deaf ears, only to the reply of something to the extent of; "now, we'll truly see what favor you have, and if it can reach you down here in this place! ...watch your fingers!" he shouted, as he proceded to shut the door on ariel.

SLAM!

-FOOT STEPS GROWING SILENT IN THE DISTANCE.

-DARK GUARD: "LIGHTS OUT!"

It then became quite apparent to ariel at that moment in time, as he lay there in "the pit" considering the circumstances staring him in the face, that he had been sentenced to death, and if he didn't find a way out of that cell (and soon), he would surely die...

And for the three days and nights (unbeknownst to him, for it was a constant pitch black night in that cell (a cell which couldn't have measured more than five meters tall and 3 meters or so in diameter). he tried through any and all means to find a way, any way... there had to be some way out. he was relentless. trying to feel his way around every inch of the room for cracks or holes, or anything which could be used to his advantage. instead only finding brittle bones and remains of it's former guests. he also tried to scale the wall, and bloodied himself by pummling his body into the cell door, but all were for not, and he being in such a physically weakend state already. he was exhausted and growing weaker still. he hadn't slept in days, nor eatten or had drink. plus being without any of his gadgets (which he had grown quite accustomed to and reliant apon), he completly had forgot all about kedar and the others at this point, as well as anak, and found it difficult to think past anything in this thick sufficating black darkness and the utter stench of death. he now was at his wits end. and had just about given up all hope.

It was in that very moment he heard something...

It was a sound very faint, but very familiar (one that he had grown quite accustomed to hearing, having been at hazar maveth for some time now. it was a sound he heard each and every night). the reason it stood out to him now, was that in the pit in which he was currntly rotting in was located in the very bowels of maveth (it was quite a journey just to reach the corridor leading to his very cell). so, for days his ears had been devoid of any noise at all (other than his weezing breaths and erratic heartbeat, which noticeably picked up with the discovery of this familiar sound).

The sound that ariel had heard, was one of a crunching noise, nibbleing and bitting... it was one of the rats (that he dreaded seeing). one of those "house rats." indeed this was very good news... he thought to himself, as the noise became louder and grew nearer. he knew if the rodent had found a way in, that he might be able to find a way out (for these were no small creatures, about the size of a fat plump cat). it was then, he could hear little bits of rubble crumbling from the wall and falling to the ground. then he realized that the rat was burrowing from the cieling, and he remembered he was too weak to reach the ceiling before, and in his current state there was no way. he didn't even know how high it stretched. if he were to have a chance he would need an extra boost of strength. then he thought back to his first night at maveth, when he was speaking to kedar and the rather shocking first impression dara had made on him, by snatching the rat off of the gound and eating it! something he could never imagine doing (not particularly fond of rats at all, tracing back to a traumatic childhood encounter... however, this is neither the time nor the place to get into such stories). he was deathly affraid (let's leave it at that, for now), but he now saw what needed to be done, he would need nourishment if he was to continue on.

The crunching noise suddenly stopped, and so did ariel... he didn't even dare to breath.

If that rat lost interest and left, it would have taken all his hopes with it.

Then much to the delight of ariel, there was a new noise, the scurrying of little foot steps. the rat was now in the room with him. quickly, ariel searched for anything he could fashion into a weapon. he checked around everwhere, still trying not to make a sound. then he felt in his lower leg pant pocket a blocky presence. he reached in and pulled out what seemed to be a book (not knowing how he could have missed it before). "that'll work!" he thought to himself. it felt surprisingly heavy for it's size. he could bearly hold it, (though he could hardly hold even himself up at this point). so, very gingerly he propped himself up in position to strike. he waited for the rat to come near to him, but it seemed to work it's way around the outter circle of the romm. then it moved back up to the ceiling (and very close to where it seemed to enter the room). "it's leaving..." he proclaimed. so without delay, with evey last ounce of strength in his body (pretty much on shear will alone), he flung that book up to the ceiling.

It made an awful thud. then three more thuds proceded it. very curious. three objects, not two (as he had hoped), not one (as he had expected) had fallen to the ground.

The book, the rat, and a large chunk of the ceiling came crashing down with them. now, sitting very still with his back to the wall. ariel was in awe of what he saw next.

a very strange single beam of light shot through the hole he had just made. however, it was a very warm and still light. it captured all his attention. his thoughts of eating and hopes of escaping had all but faded away into the deeper recesses of his mind. there was only he, the light... this magnificent light. but what was this brilliant light, that seeemed to thrill and calm him all at once?

after gazing in the light for some time... and what seemed like either a few seconds or what could have been several hours. ariel moved into the light. he assumed it could be the sun (but having never seen the sun he could not say for sure). but if that indeed was sunlight he was standing in. this would be no small accurance in itself. infact, it would have been history making... a miracle even. but what caused the sun to breakthrough that barrier that had blocked it all these years? and in addition to that, how had it reached him there in the pit (which could have been hundreds of meters below the surface, perhaps more, he thought). all this didn't make too much sense to him as it happend. he began to wonder if he had 'lost it' and if he was hallucinating, or perhaps even... had he died? it was just then, as all these thoughts began to race in his head that he looked down where the light hit the ground, and he snapped back into reality as he had seen the rat that he had slain and the open book that lay directly adjacent to it. then without hesitation he kneeled down to pick up not the dead carcas that he had previously hungered for, but instead the book that he previously had no interest in.

once ariel picked up the book and began to read, again the concept of time escaped him, and he lost all track of it. he quickly, but methodically went through the book, cover to cover. then, as if it were illuminated by his reading, the light faded out, just as he had finished. not fully understanding what happend, and what would happen next for that matter. ariel began to pray (half applying what he had just learned from the reading and half out of uncertainty about what was happening inside of him). never having prayed before this came surprisingly easy to him. he felt fully comfortale with speaking to God. it seemed to come naturally. he conversed for hours and hours and seemed content on going on and on without end, but he had to stop, when he was interrupted by that great light which had returned again. he had no delay in grabbing the book and reading through it yet again. and once more as he had finished it (like clockwork) the light went out again. this was an ongoing event that happend forty times in total. each time he read through the book a different story or chapter reached out and grabbed him it seemed new (even on the fortieth). it just so happend that on the fortieth time as he was in the middle of his read for that

day (caught up in the eleventh chapter of the last book, i believe), when the light suddenly went out! "hmmm.. most curious." he said aloud. immediatly following that statement the latch on his cell door loudly became undone. as another beam of light shot in through the crack. however, this time a very artificial and cold beam.

then as the door slowly creaked open... all goes black and he collapses to the ground. just seeing blurry silhouettes before passing out

Chapter Three
Dawn
of the way

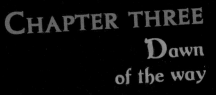

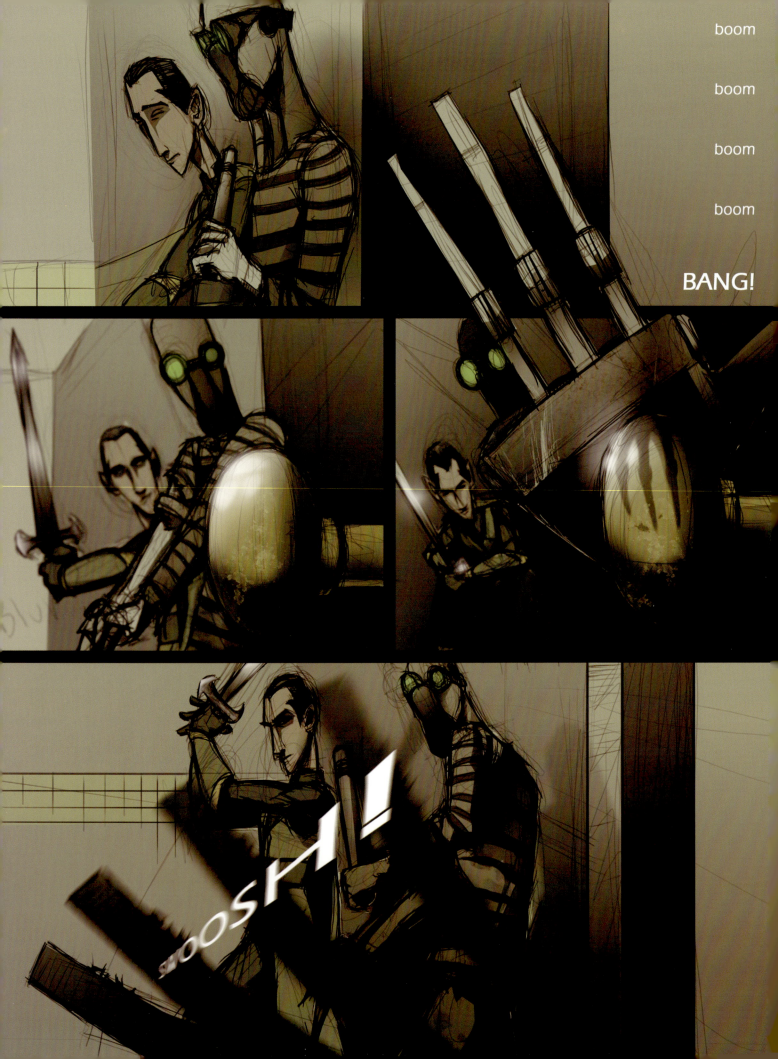

As the group quickly made their way as far from the encampment as possible (not wanting to run into any more of elymas' guards, traps or sentries), they were delayed by other prisoners who sought them out for help. for many of the prisoners were no more deserving of being locked up than you or i, having been unjustly accused and made (for the most part) slaves so many years...knew of not much else. not knowing how to function in the world beyond those prison gates. being now freed, they truly did not know what to do with that new found freedom and for all purposes were lost. so, logically they wanted to 'tag' along with those from the "outside world" who have saved them and brought them what they had been praying for for years now. many pledging their allegiance to ariel and zeb. also, not wanting to turn their backs on any people in need (needless to say, these people, many who ariel had grown to know and became quite fond of and vise versa), the group welcomed their new guest on this ever slowing journey...for they were stopping every few minutes with new people "coming on board." this delayed their travel considerably, having to welcome and greet new commers and answer questions about where they were headed and what had happend (for some still did not know, they just ran at first sign of opportunity), and thus and so forth (this also prevented ariel and zeb from getting reacquainted) and seemed to go on for Several hours...

...however this would not be the last they would see of elymas and his guards

The following journal entries are excerpts from dalphon's accounts of the days following the escape (only the events that are of immediate significance have been included, the census and catalogging of "new additions" have been excluded, as well scenerios that will later be visited).

september 12, the sky grows dark, but press on we do for press on we must. 'no time to stop now,' ariel and zeb have both been very adament about us either finding shelter or making contact with the others before that avenue would even be considered. but thus far, nothing. not a mountain or hill or even a tumble weed to speak of. nothing...nothing but flat, dead earth. kedar and zeb have nerues pulling double duty now, he is still attempting to reach the rest of the rescue team (that was our supposed transport out of this wretched place), but in addition he has now become kedar's own personal lamp, lighting the way...the flock has grown quite tired now... i don't even know how many hours now that we've been in non-stop transit, but without a doubt this has been the longest and most trying portion of this entire mission, and it shows no signs of letting up. but i shant worry for i know we are in good hands, and i do believe that all is taken care of, for the favor is with us and all will be well in the end.

september 14, morning, yes morning...finally. last night was quite awful. awfly uneventfull, that is. still no sign of anything, nor word from the others. thank God for the morning light, nerues has been running low on his fuel cells for quite sometime now, and has needed to replenish his batteries as well. zeb has taken him off of "lamp duty" and will soley have him focus on "radio duties" and sparingly at that (at least while his batteries recharge). i do so hope we find some form of shelter by nightfall. we stumbled apon quite a few new commers today. though, i haven't had the opportunity to tally them all up just yet. kedar says these are some of the hardest working men and women that he has had the pleasure of working besides. however, thus far they have been most fond of complaining. i feel nerves running thin. i don't know how much longer we can go on like this.

september 15, group moral is currently very low, just last night we suffered a bit of a disapointment, as we believed to have found a spot of shelter to recoop ourselves (in the ruins of what seemed to be a former great city), but before i even had a moment to take off my boots or lose my knickers, dara jumped down from her look-out post. reporting of a small (but more than formidable) patrol of lotan's soldiers that were doing a sweep of the ruined city... so, yet again on the move we found ourselves. seems that the longer we travel and the further we seemed to go,

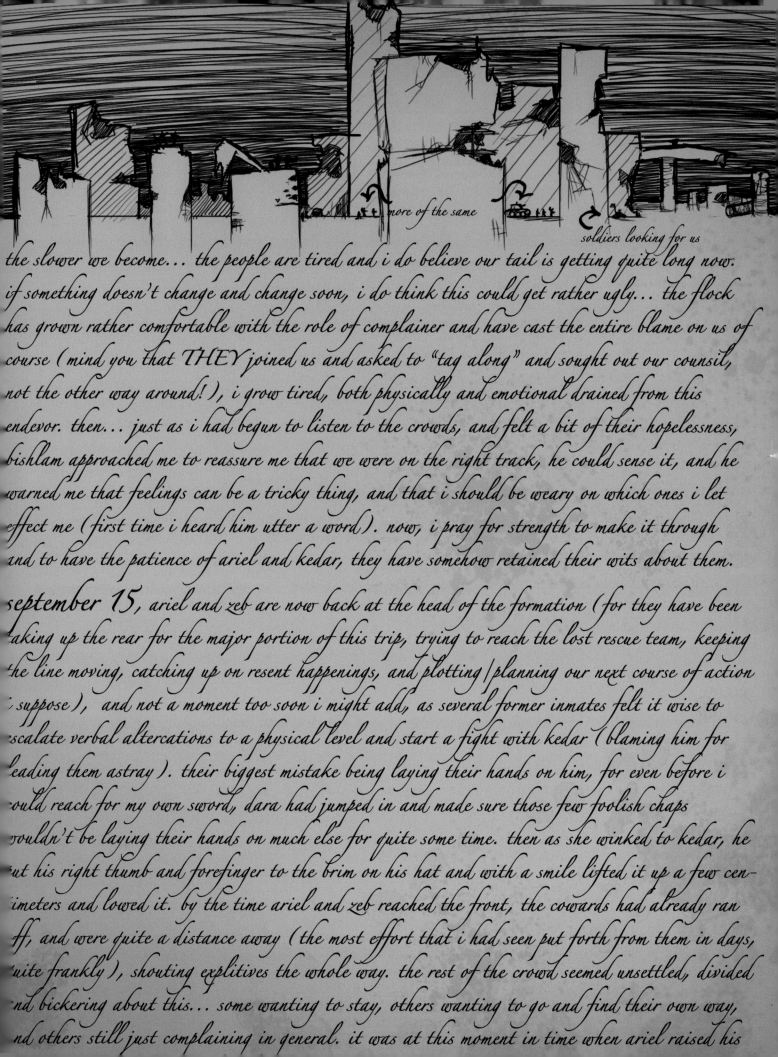

more of the same

soldiers looking for us

the slower we become... the people are tired and i do believe our tail is getting quite long now. if something doesn't change and change soon, i do think this could get rather ugly... the flock has grown rather comfortable with the role of complainer and have cast the entire blame on us of course (mind you that THEY joined us and asked to "tag along" and sought out our counsil, not the other way around!), i grow tired, both physically and emotional drained from this endevor. then... just as i had begun to listen to the crowds, and felt a bit of their hopelessness, bishlam approached me to reassure me that we were on the right track, he could sense it, and he warned me that feelings can be a tricky thing, and that i should be weary on which ones i let effect me (first time i heard him utter a word). now, i pray for strength to make it through and to have the patience of ariel and kedar, they have somehow retained their wits about them.

september 15, ariel and zeb are now back at the head of the formation (for they have been taking up the rear for the major portion of this trip, trying to reach the lost rescue team, keeping the line moving, catching up on resent happenings, and plotting/planning our next course of action i suppose), and not a moment too soon i might add, as several former inmates felt it wise to escalate verbal altercations to a physical level and start a fight with kedar (blaming him for leading them astray). their biggest mistake being laying their hands on him, for even before i could reach for my own sword, dara had jumped in and made sure those few foolish chaps wouldn't be laying their hands on much else for quite some time. then as she winked to kedar, he put his right thumb and forefinger to the brim on his hat and with a smile lifted it up a few centimeters and lowed it. by the time ariel and zeb reached the front, the cowards had already ran off, and were quite a distance away (the most effort that i had seen put forth from them in days, quite frankly), shouting explitives the whole way. the rest of the crowd seemed unsettled, divided and bickering about this... some wanting to stay, others wanting to go and find their own way, and others still just complaining in general. it was at this moment in time when ariel raised his

hand (the metal one) to quiet the mob, and addressed them as follows (best as i can recall):
"do not fret! this road has been a long and trying one… but fear not, rather be confident. not conformed to environment around you, but instead transformed by a renued spirit in the good news… before days end we shall reach our long awaited target."
(sounded better when he said it, i think) no one seemed to question this, but having heard these words we all felt a smidge better. and everyone pushed forward, finding the strength to continue on with peace and renewed confidence and resolve. and to say it right, i felt quite jolly.

september 15, now as things finally seemed to be looking up, i walked at the front with ariel and zeb and overheard a bit of their conversation. a conversation that i only caught the tai end of, but i could tell it was one of importance (cause both zeb and ariel had very stern and serious faces when the spoke) one name kept popping up, loatn, sethur lotan a believe. it was definitely a political topic and zeb was telling ariel of his power and presence and how it was growing in the east (and not in a good way mind you). suddenly, the topic changed (possibly on account of my presence) and zeb was telling ariel of the MANY failed atempts of rescuing him from hazar maveth (i can attest that there were at least 3 attempts, just in my short tenier with the group), one of the last being the planting of anak as a rouge guard. which ariel proclaimed that now things were starting to make sense to him and spoke of the foiled mine shaft escape attempt. as zeb went on to the last ditch effort (which seemed to be the sum of all previous plans) going over the details of the tacticle aspects of the raid and as she spoke of this she paused and had a rather sad look about her. then mentioned the "fine mess" that this had become with them being lost in this desert wilderness (in a much lower voice, just short of a whisper), and all the months that she wasn't able to save ariel as he rotted away in that wicked place. sr continued on to apologize that she wasn't as good a leader as he, and that if she had been, may this whole situation would have never happend… and that was when ariel cut her off, saying; "faith z. after all these years of you showing me how faith opperates. now, more than ever is when we need faith the most." he saw hope, a hope that was made possible by her efforts, her leading this team, to do what had never been done, ever. he wouldn't change this situation one bit, from begining to end all things had happened for a reason. then he reminded her that it was HIS foolish actions (not hers) that started this mess in the first place. she chimed in, saying, but if i could have saved you earlier, it… he cut her off again, saying; but you have saved me,

…in more ways then you could know. much has happend to me in hazar. something extradinary. there was this light and… and… eyes where opened… my eyes. now i see. i believe…yes now i believe. then there was a rather wonderful silence (the sort that i feel you would have to be there to entirely understand and appreciate). and i do believe that if i could see their eyes at that moment, that they would have been big and full of tears. after that long delay, zeb said (with a smerk of smile on her face) i knewed you'd come around sooner or later… she was interrupted yet again, but this time it was from the people behind them. for now the sun had began to set and the land was as flat as it had ever been. the people began to shout, and yell lamenting over their perril. they screamed, "you snakes! you've tricked us, sentenced us all to death, you have! we were better off in maveth!" just then zeb had spotted someting on her scope in the distance, she prclaimed; "there is a pretrusion from the horizon directly north of us!" this quieted the shouting, but murmers continued. so, we continued north and now we all can now see what zeb had seen. we should reach it in a matter of mere hours. but alas, it grows dark. so i will continue writing when light is adaquet.

by gum! doesn't look like much but it's the most pleasent sight this trip trip

september 16, as we all made way towards the "earthly pertrusion" when we arrived we all took notice to what appered to be more like a small cluster of mountains (a very dark rugged and not the least bit inviting cluster). ariel and zeb assessed the situation, and realized that in their current state, the company we had accumilated could not scale this massive wall (even the best of our core group would have a challenging struggle to reach the top). and we couldn't set up camp here, for if lotans troops or bounty hunters caught up with us here we were done for (or as ariel put it "caught between a rock and a hard place."). so we all agreed to go around even though it was a far longer trek, it was a neccessary course of action. and to no one's suprise the crumbling commenced; "we are hungry, we are thirsty, we are (fill in the blank)."

never the less, as we begain to move around this huge rock, they proceded to follow again. then, a voice over the groanings shouted out; "wait! hold on you guys. i can do it. i can make it over to the other side." it was vashti (who had to push her way to reach the front of the line). ariel replied; "to what avail? the rest can not." "i can go across and see if it safe. from here we have no idea what is on the other side. we could be walking into a trap for all we know. i can bring a transmitter and signal nerues if all is clear... c'mon ariel, you know i'm right." said she. "very well." ariel replied. then out of nowhere zeb points to me and says; "dalphon, go with vas. watch out for her... you two be careful now." "see you on the other side." added ariel. so there we split from the group, 'wild' vashti and myself, moving up this unknown treacherous incline while the others went around. the climb itself went fairly well and we scaled it suprisingly easily, and in good time. along the way we wondered what would happen next. plans falling apart left and right, being lost in a foriegn hostile land persued by trained professional killers. hadn't the foggiest of how deep we were in it (it's strange how fear and doubt can really do a number on your head). the rest trip spent in idle chatter, trying to cheer one another up, but as we approached the top of the mountain, conversations came to a halt. as images of what lay on the other side of that ridge danced in our heads. finally, as we stood there and piered over the edge, neither of us could have been prepared for what we were about to see. a mountain side like non we had ever seen. it was directly across from us on the other side, a valley seperating us from it. it stood as tall as the one in which we stood (couldn't have been a hundred meters away), but it was full of holes and looked very much like a chunk of swiss cheese. and as we made our way down we noticed this side of the mountain was really quite smooth. unlike the the side we had just traversed up and very much different from the side we were looking across to. as we made our way further down we both heard an odd sound (odd because niether of us could place it at first), and for a second both of us stopped. a rather pequiller sound it was, much like a crackling noise, then more like a pouring or spilling noise. then we looked down in amazed wonderment. for i was seeing something that my eyes had never seen prior to this moment... it was a stream... a stream of water, all bright as glass, a small but glorious stream that ran in the valley between the two superstructures. we both ran down, and as we made our way down, just kneeling to draw a sip, i noticed vashti had stopped, so i did as well. she said a short prayer of thanks and i bowed my head with her. then without any further delay i offered to test the water and see if it was really proper for drinking, and i drank. i say! never before have i tasted a water so sweet. vashti gladly joined in. as i drank i felt stronger, you needent drink much of it, for it quenched your thirst at once, absolutly delightful! another strange thing was that as i searched to where the water came from, it seemed to run out of a rock in the center of these two opposing mountains and disappear into another rock on the opposite side of the revine. immediately after our drink we both split up to check the surrounding area. we worked our way to the other mountain across from us and checked each of "holes" in the mountain side. they actually turned out being rather quiant little caves and caverns varying in size and shape, but most measuring no more than ten meters deep and three wide and just a bit shorter than then i (as i had to crowch down each time carful not to hit my head). as we searched we found nothing, they were all completly empty and what originally seemed to be man made dwellings, at a closer look had no traces of such handywork. they seemed to be a natural occurance of the rock formation. we then signaled nereus that the cost was clear (just as we thought we had searched every nook and cranny), but it appeared that we spoke too soon, for we stumbled apon another opening, one that we hadn't seen before, it was much larger than the others and was deeper as well. it appeard to be a passage. a long corridor leading some where. we followed this narrow pathway in a thick black darkness that you could feel on your face. and as we made our way through this clostrophobic path it opened up into much larger yet still pitch dark room. the air was crisp and sweet (much like the water) my eyes grew large as they strained to see a small light that was above us, that was also about a hundred meters away. the light was very dim and hard to make out. it was useless in shedding any light on the room we were in, or how large it was, or what was in the room with us (for i felt presence there other than us). just then we both heard a noise coming from that dim light. suddenly it got so bright it was nearly blinding, though squint we did not, niether did i blink. for what i now saw had arrested all of my attention. out called a voice; "yo! you guys down there?" it was nereus. but for the life of me i could not reply, i couldn't even speak. for sitting not ten steps from us was a mountain of a tree.

at first glance i thought i perhaps that i was hulucinating (that maybe there was something in the water). for, i had only seen pictures of trees and heard of a few wealthy politicians who ha owned the only known gardens that remained and of course i had heard the tales of the wicked dead forrests, but this was a real, alive and breathing, full and healthy, fruitbearing tree. not mentioning the fact that it was growing forth in the center of a cave!

september 17, last night as ariel and zeb caught up to us, the flock entered the cavern in groves to see this "supposed" tree. and much to thier shock and awe, as nerues shined the light again on the massive... tree (i say just "tree" because i couldn't tell the sort, nor could anyone else), it was a tree of unkown class or age. dara was proclaimed that this was no ordinary tre and it wasn't just some fluke that it had grown here, and survived all these years. "centuries old." she was convinced. "finally... dara, we have found... something that is... older... than you!" joked anak (yelling from the opening of the cavern, for he could not fit through the passage). a statement that i am not entirely sure to be true (no one knows for sure dara's age, but what i do know is that she is the oldest and wisest person that i have ever met, and that is saying a lot. considering i only met her a few days prior). after the initial awe had worn off, the people began to leap up and climb the tree. ariel immediatly rebuked them, commanding that they control their flesh, for there were others in the group that were quite ill and should be first attended to, and that it was a matter of respect. when ariel spoke people listened. he has an ever so chilling authoritative presence. they relented, and we all stood eagerly awaiting (though, i feel the rest of the core group was more than apprehensive about eating friut from a strange tree for all together seperate reasons). then dara said the most beautiful prayer as she blessed the food. and as she said amen, ariel walked over to the tree and grabbed the friut (without even standing on his tip toes, for he was tall enough to reach the branches and didn't need to jump or climb on the tree) and handed it down. dara was the first to eat, then kedar, and zeb and so on and so forth (i believe it was dispersed from eldest to youngest, and then shared with our eager guests). it all was run decently and in order, no pushing shoving or fighting. there we all sat, eating till we had enough and could not eat any more. and this was the first time i had seen smiles on many of these new faces. it was a quite jolly time for all! this was truly worth the journey, there was laughing and cheering, everyone made a joyful noise, in one way or another. i rested my eyes, for what i thought to only be a second, but as i looked up i noticed that everyone had dozed off underneath the tree (not that i could see them entirely, hardly distinguishing the rocks from the figures, the room was very dimly lit, by the glowing lights from nerues' charging cells). it was dead quiet (something that my ears were quite thanful for, having been marred for days with bickering and complaining). i got up and made my way carfully towards the corridor, to see who was on watch. to my surprise there were MANY others asleep outside in the exterior dwellings. kedar had been posted at the entrance of the tunnel, vashti and dara atop each peak of each mountain tops, giant anak was reclining at the base of one of the mountains, with his legs flat against the ground and is his back flat to the incline of the mountain (like a huge stone chair), with chloe not far away (of course), sleeping under one of the folds in his poncho (all together looking much like an absurdly oversized man child with a small toy doll), and the rest scattered about. a handfull here, a cluster there, all at rest and in the utmost peaceful dream state imaginable. and in the middle of it all ariel and zeb sat, in deep meditation and prayer... not wanting to disturb them i returned underground (not finding a single vaccant cave). i sat next to kedar in the doorway of the tunnel. we spoke briefly, not that i remember any of that conversation. for as soon as i sat down, my eyelids became too heavy to keep open. next thing i knew, it was morning.

Minutes before sunrise ariel and zebuddah are the only two still awke. they sit in the silence seeking guidence in this great time of need. many questions, but few answers; what happened to the rest of the rescue team? should they continue their search for them, or should they consider the possibility of staying in this oasis? was it too good to pass up, or was this place even safe to stay in? surely, elymas would find them here, his forces couldn't miss a place like this, could they? but then again, it seems virtually untouched, and uninhabbited, how could a place like this, go on so many years and be undiscovered? perhaps it was all a trap? they prayed together in one accord for the first time as brother and sister. they prayed for guidance and direction, wisdom, knowledge, and understanding over fear and doubt. as their prayer came to an end they opened their eyes looking eastward, and the first thing they saw was a new shinning sun rising (almost completely white and at least three times its normal size). secondly, they looked up at a sky so blue (bluer than either of them knew it could be), without a cloud in sight. there they sat, still, taken aback for a moment, and almost in disbelief of the what they were seeing next. more impacted by the third thing they were seeing than the previous two...because now what they were seeing caught all their attention, for one by one, the people popped out of their dwellings, all the followers that they had accumulated along the way to this miracle in the desert and they were great in number (far greater than formerly expected). out they came rubbing the sleep out of their eyes. even they theirselves couldn't believe what they were seeing. in every direction you even more poured out of the cavern where the tree layed, this more than double the already daunting number. and as this awesome event unfolded it became all to clear (even clearer than the sky) what ariel and zebuddah were here to do.

i didn't even know there were this many people in hazar!

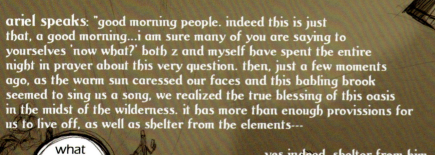

ariel speaks: "good morning people. indeed this is just that, a good morning...i am sure many of you are saying to yourselves 'now what?' both z and myself have spent the entire night in prayer about this very question. then, just a few moments ago, as the warm sun caressed our faces and this babling brook seemed to sing us a song, we realized the true blessing of this oasis in the midst of the wilderness. it has more than enough provisions for us to live off, as well as shelter from the elements---

what about elymas!?

yes indeed, shelter from him and his forces as well, do we find in this land. does the word not say that no weapon formed against us shall prosper? and that your God shall provide all your needs? well, surely this is that provision, and as far as elymas, we needen't be worried with him any longer, even if the persuers do come, we will be ready for them!

this land is good and plentiful we will fashion it inot two colonies. the first tikvath, (which means foundation) it's inhabitants will live in the mountain's surface dwellings, and will be responsible for the security of both colonies, to watch and protect, if need be." **zebuddah speaks:** "the secondcolony will be called tiria, (which means hope), since by God's grace we were given hope in this place. the people in this group will live underground in the caverns sourounding the great tree. these people will be responsible for provisions for both colonies, food and water consumption, distribution and up keep. we see the potential here for a great God blessed community. but nothing will be achieved without unity, and us allbeing on one accord."

ariel: "times like this i am reminded of an old song that i have just recently leared:

i will sing to the LORD for he has triumphed gloriously. who is like you, o LORD, among the gods? who is like You, glorious in holiness, fearful in praises, doing wonders? You in Your mercy have led forth the people whom You have redeemed; You have guided them in Your strength to Your holy habitation. the people will hear and be afraid; sorrow will take hold of the inhabitants of maacah, then the cheifs of hazar maveth will be dismayed; the mighty men of the wicked forrests, trembling will take hold of them; all the inhabitants of evil city will melt away. fear and dread will fall on them by the greatness of Your arm they will be as still as a stone. till your people pass over, o LORD, till the people pass over whom You have purchased. You will bring them in and plant them in the mountain of Your inheritance, in the place, o LORD, which You have made for Your own dwelling, sanctuary, o LORD, which Your hands have established...

the LORD shall reign for ever and ever!"

who is with us!?!

for tiria and tikvath!

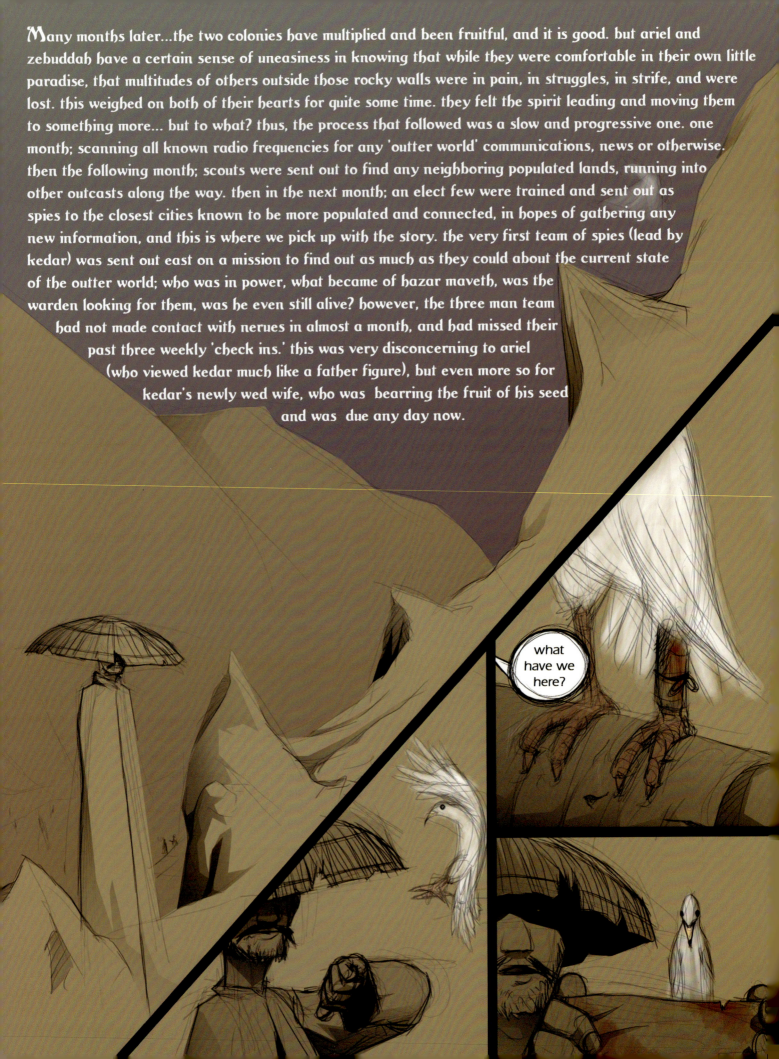

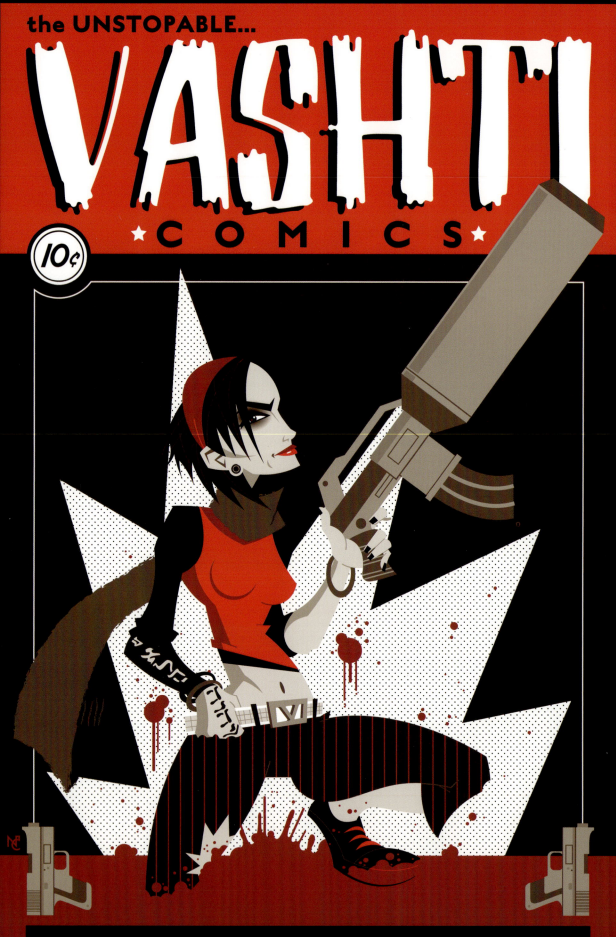

guest artists **philip perales** www.whosdaboss.net

guest artists **tayen kim** www.starkat.org

Special Thanks to:

God the Father: to whom all credit is due.
The Holy Spirit: for the vision, for the ability, for the strength.
Christ Jesus: for salvation. Without which I would be lost and this project dead.
He is my all in all.

Parents James and Fely Conner: whose support made this all possible. I am forever grateful. Also, for raising such a thoughtful, kind, caring, and amazingly well adjusted young man :¬p

To the rest. Friends, family, and godsends: Nic Cowan, Philip Perales, Tayen Kim, Monique Cowan, Jeff Conner, pastor Fred Price jr., Donivan Howard, Richard Guiton, Harvey Cloyd, Analisse De Lara, Amy "da juice" and the Philadelphia street team, Hana Wood and Skip from typecraft, Steve Mok and Gi Sook from black market LB, Brian Taylor from Pnuma books, Otis college of art and design, Mike and John Anderson from tankfarm, LC and Michele from cannibal flower, and lastly all the long beach town center crew (past and present).

you all lended a helping hand, opened a door when needed. your support won't be forgotten and will always be much appreciated. you hold a special place in my heart all of you. thanks, i love you more than you could know.

guest artists **monique cowan** thephlypsyde@yahoo.com

"Dara"

in the name of Jesus

I represent the outcasts, the radicals,
the remnant
We are the only ones who will outlast
Cuz he who outlasts
Will inherit salvation
-through degradation and persecution
but we have the revelation of
Revolution
razing seducing spirits
while crying out the rebel yell so
the world can hear it—
"Hallelujah!"
cuz we tryin' to get through to the
masses
and his wrath is our mission
while fishing for men
and then we can march into the
new city
and dwell with the Lord
but for now, we've been given a
great sword
to fight with that great whore
Babylon
And we travel on
to get the next battle on
make sure we saddle on our armor
lest we walk naked and be shamed
cuz we have Good News to proclaim
and we've got to exalt his name
-and if the truth hurts,
then we've come to bring the pain
to those who exchange the truth
of the sane doctrine
for the lie
and been made drunk with the wine
of the whore's fornication
cuz we have the revelation of
revolution
the solution to the ills
the antidote for the blue pill
the revelation of Revolution
cuz it's raining revolution.
Jesus is the Reigning Revolution.